METAL EARTH

JUDAS SYNDROME

Cover and format design created by Glaring Productions.

Printed on acid free paper.

Second Edition

ISBN 978-0-6152-3984-2

ACKNOWLEDGMENTS

I would like to dedicate this book to my friends and family, especially my little sister who helped out along the way with editing and suggesting some great story details.

This book also couldn't have been accomplished without my love for science-fiction. Hopefully my book can live up to the high standards set by previous epics.

METAL EARTH

JUDAS SYNDROME

Daniel J. Wente

A Glaring Productions Publication

TABLE OF CONTENTS:

Intro: A New Start 9

Chapter 1: Return from Big Blue 13

Chapter 2: Danger, Danjerr 25

Chapter 3: Darker Shadows 35

Chapter 4: Backdoor Meeting 41

Chapter 5: Fuel for Thought 47

Chapter 6: Inauguration 59

Chapter 7: Division.....and Math 69

Chapter 8: Don't Forget About Veeson 77

Chapter 9: To Stalk a Hunter 87

Chapter 10: Who's Who? 95

Chapter 11: No Water 105

Chapter 12: Mending Wounds 117

Codex: Locations 123

People/Groups/Entities 124

Weapons/Technology 126

INTRO:

A NEW START

The daylight from dawn doesn't signal a brand new day anymore. In fact, those days are only remembered by the elder citizens of Space Station OI-0, or as its referred to by all humans, Oyioh. Oyioh is one of four space stations that orbits the now defunct planet earth. These other civilized satellites are Akyria (KR-7), Ikoss (EK-X), and Veeson (VS-1). The group of stations is commonly referred to as 'Metal Earth' to distinguish it from the locations on earth.

These habitable stations were created by the United States government originally as space fortresses to combat any aerial or nuclear attack on U.S. soil. However, this idea was short-lived when Earth was defenseless against a barrage of meteors that struck in the year 2056. Those rich enough or with the right connections were able to board ships and create new lives on these stations. The entire Ikoss station was bought out by the Russians, a regret Americans don't forget. Wealthy and politically powerful Europeans made it onto Veeson. The approximate population total of all four stations is only about 74,000.

Earth isn't entirely deserted though as many try to survive the toxic gases. Current estimates place the survivor count at about 2 million. Anarchy was created when all organized government left for space enabling crime lords to fill that void. Some survivors do try to sneak aboard ships that periodically come back to earth to strip it for resources. However, such actions were made illegal to prevent contaminants coming into

the Metal Earth stations. Deportation is a lucky outcome for

illegal passengers who are more likely to face death.

Each space station has it's own government in place and

due to obvious lack of supplies and resources there is little trust

between governments, even the two dominantly American

stations, Oyioh and Akyria.

CHAPTER 1:

RETURN FROM

BIG BLUE

It's roughly 1900 hour. Military time has replaced usual civilian time due to artificial light and lack of consistent light hours on the space stations since humans no longer have the rotation of the earth to serve as day and night. The USS Avalon, formerly one of the greatest vessels in the American fleet before it was reinvented as a freighter-fighter, has returned from earth with some much needed fossil fuels, lumber, and other minerals.

The ship's men are decked out in teal fatigues with slate colored armor, some with heavy weapons, some with just handguns. A dark-haired pilot, Michael Stall, appears less armored but displays many awards along the sleeve of his jacket. And then there's the apparent authority figure, Captain Jaren Lee. Jaren isn't much of an opposing figure for someone with such high command. He is only average size if not slightly overweight. A scruffy five o'clock shadow covers his face, a look that will cease upon his arrival at the Oyioh Citadel. Compensating for his lack of intimidation is his customized weapon of choice. It was handed down to him from his father who was a weapon-smith. Around the system it's known as the Ranlian Reaper. The weapon is a one-man army equipped with dual photon pistols and a grenade launcher just above the scythe blade that encircles the handle. It is rarely used by the peace-minded Captain Lee who remembers seeing his hometown of Minsteria crushed by a failed coup of the Oyioh government. That rebel elitist group is known as the "Change for Progress."

This anarchist group, also called the "Progs," was currently in power of the U.S. until the meteor strike hit. The rebel group lost their power due to the control the military had setting up the new government on the space stations. The Progs have tried to end the ban on illegal passengers from earth in exchange for their support to help overtake the current government. Their thirst for power blinds them from realizing the risk of radiation and overpopulation they bring to Metal Earth. It's a move that would only replicate the crippling effect of earth onto the new homes of Americans.

A recent trip to earth resulted in a heated debate between Jaren and Michael. As the crew was about to load up and take off back for Oyioh, a young woman with a child tried to sneak onboard before being discovered by Michael. Jaren came around and demanded the two people to access the Decontamination Center and apply for citizenship legally and wait their turn like everyone else. However, the two visibly scarred survivors resisted before Michael pulled out his gun and shot them dead.

Jaren, the captain, was upset with Michael's actions, but Michael remains firm on his stance to protect his new home, Metal Earth, from any unknown outside threats. The two friends have since cooled on the subject when it was revealed later that another excavation team was murdered by bitter stowaways who planned on ramming the freighter into a space station. The freighter was effectively shot down by Akyrian mercenaries.

The usually calm Captain Jaren Lee paces around and commands Pilot Michael Stall to dock the ship on Oyioh. The crew is small and it's their last recovery mission for the month. As the ship nestles into the bay, Jaren peers through the window to see his girlfriend, Janah Omen, waiting for him. Jaren reaches into his pocket and pulls out a box and opens it. It's the ring he's been waiting months to give to Janah. As his mind drifts into those thoughts they are interrupted abruptly.

Michael Stall shouts to Jaren on the bridge "The Avalon is docked sir, all systems are offline and personnel exiting may commence."

Jaren doesn't hear the announcement as he is in too much of his own world that he notices nothing but Janah, a frail blond diplomat, waiting outside. Michael again calls out, "Sir, we can..."

Jaren cuts him off "Commence personnel exiting."

The small crew all exit as men on the exterior begin unloading the cargo hold. When Jaren makes his way off the brightly-lit steel ramp he looks desperately for Janah. Finally, he spots her behind the crowd of onlookers and begins to make his way over to her. Jaren navigates through some people but gets about only ten steps in before he is immediately cut off by Senator Jopalmin, who is due to take his presidential oath in a matter of days for Oyioh. He will be only the third president of the American Alliance.

Senator Jopalmin, a rather pudgy man dressed in ceremonial attire as usual, thinks rather highly of himself and less of anyone else. The paleness of his skin is rivaled only by that of his clothing. His curly blond hair and goatee are clean cut and his overall appearance seems artificial. A young hip look that doesn't bother to defy his age. Jopalmin will become President of the American Alliance in a couple of days at the age of 37.

"Thanks for your service Captain Lee. We are most grateful for your speedy return. The higher-ups here are certainly glad you're working for us and not those damn Akyrians. However, I do have one last request before you take your scheduled service leave." Says the senator.

Senator Jopalmin guides Jaren along with him and away from his guards and Janah to deliver the news, "Our intelligence states that the Akyrians have discovered some new element in their latest excavation to earth and it is apparently a very efficient fuel, *very* efficient. Which means good news for you and your crew. You wouldn't need to make near as many excavation trips for fuel. Jaren, we must get that element from them. They're calling it Metal Earth's Savior. They're calling it 'Zionium.'"

Jaren replies, "Why can't we just work with them? Senator Gellar can be a reasonable guy. This Zionium element would be beneficial for both of us. With fuel sources low for everyone, we need to cooperate. ”

Jopalmin, growing a little furious, responds, “Don't you think we would be in talks now if Gellar were the good person you say he *seems* to be? Look, I need you to do this with your crew and I need you to leave for Akyria by the morning.”

Jaren responds, “I just want to get back to my family, friends, and my girlfriend. I am scheduled for a month off and I plan on taking it!” Jaren tries to walk away but he is stopped after he turns around by Jopalmin's guards.

Jopalmin speaks up, “You know, if you complete this task and we get that element, it would mean less excavation trips which would naturally mean more time off for yourself.”

Jaren, now frustrated realizing he has few options, asks “What time does the USS Avalon depart?”

Jopalmin smirks and happily states “0800 hour, I will make your crew, the docks, and the Avalon's maintenance team aware of the situation.”

It looks like Jaren will have to wait a little bit longer on that wedding proposal. Jaren makes his way to find Janah in a more gloomy mood than he had originally planned. The crowd has now since dispersed and Janah is not in sight. Suddenly, Jaren's comm messages him, its Janah, she's in the military instillation's food court. Jaren finds his way to a glitzy table with Janah cracking a smile as Jaren finds his seat.

"What took so long?" inquires Janah.

"Jeez, I'm gone for two weeks, threes days earlier than normal, and you ask what took so long?" Jaren fires back with a bit of sarcasm.

The two share a laugh until Jaren breaks the news after a deep sigh, "Janah.....I...I can't stay long."

Janah immediately responds "Why not? What's wrong?"

Jaren reluctantly responds, "They want me and the crew to go on one last mission before break.....to Akyria."
Janah asks, "Akyria?! What for? There has never been anything but trouble when you go there."

Jaren tries to make things easier saying, "It shouldn't take long. It's a basic trip, and when we get back we'll be on break for longer periods of time. They promise."

Janah angrily points out "Senator Jopalmin promises a lot of things which he never delivers."

At that moment, there's a loud crash right into the food court damaging the corner of museum tower on it's way down. Civilians begin to panic and scramble as nearby guards come to investigate. Debris flies within forty yards of Jaren and Janah as dust quickly plumes into their eyes. It appears to be an Akyrian Cruiser, but the Akyrian markings are partially scratched off, possibly a result of the crash. Two men jump out and take off through the adjacent corridor. The surrounding smoke covers their leave. Sirens are sounding off and soldiers arrive at the scene and surround the vessel. After a few verbal warnings, the soldiers move into the ship finding just a dead pilot and a destroyed maintenance droid. A recovery team now joins the scene and retrieves four cases of spices and two crates of canned goods. There are no weapons or any other signs of other

passengers found. The pilot has no identification on him and the

droid's memory circuits are fried.

Jaren and Janah have now brushed themselves off after a

few moments. They avoid the debris and walk over to crash

scene.

Jaren asks, "Found anything?"

The recovery chief answers "Nothing serious captain. It

appears to be nothing more than a small freighter transporting

some food."

Senator Jopalmin comes in from the back and interjects,

"Since when does Akyria use Cruiser ships as freighters? Never.

The answer is never. There's more to it than this, I believe the

Akyrians are aware that we know about their secret and so

they've sent a spy disguised as a merchant."

Jaren responds, "That's quite an assumption sir, I don't

think we can jump to conclusions like that. We don't even know

why or how that ship crashed into here."

"We *do* know why it crashed here and we're gonna investigate this to the fullest. Get your crew ready captain, we now need you to leave immediately." Jopalmin responds.

After a brief pause, Jaren aks, "How do we know why this ship crashed?"

Jopalmin states, "It was trespassing."

Jaren asks, "Trespassing?"

Jopalmin, short on details, says, "Yes, trespassing."

Jaren grows curious, "We shot them down?"

Senator delivers a forceful message, "Just make sure your crew is out and on its way to Akyria in two hours. Our time is less than we thought. If they're aware of this, your mission may be rougher than planned. Make sure your men are armed and the USS Avalon weaponry is functional. Good luck captain."

Jaren interrupts, "But, sir."

Jopalmin quickly and sternly ends the conversation "*Good* day captain!"

CHAPTER 2:

DANGER, DANJERR

It's near midnight, but the sun is still present and will be
out for several more days, not good for someone on the run and
trying to stay in the shadows. These same people hiding are the
same two who escaped the crash scene. Two blond Akyrians,
Danjerr Ohm and Aren K'Napp. Aren is hobbled by a sprained
ankle and is now a liability for Danjerr, a former Oyiohan soldier
turned mercenary. The two are dressed in similar black and blues
with light armor covered by cloaks. Danjerr's only injury

appears to be a slight cut on the side of his forehead where Akyrians mark there citizens with various tattoos. Danjerr received his tattoo after his defection, not at birth like Aren.

Aren addresses Danjerr, "You must go on and get the element, I'm only gonna slow you down now. I'll cover you with a diversion so you can get another ship out of here."

Danjerr states, "Um, there's a problem with that strategy. I need a pilot. Remember? Those damn Oyiohan guards have Austin and MZX-20, if they even survived the crash."

"You're resourceful. Figure something out. Remember our trip to Veeson when you talked the Imperial guard into letting us leave because we were on a fact-finding mission for the Council of Strategic Defenses, a council that doesn't even exist!" answers Aren.

"Yeah, that was a pretty good one, huh. Alright, but take care of yourself, I'll be coming back for you." Danjerr responds and then activates his cloaking apparel, or as he affectionately refers to as the "Cloak of Shadows," a name Danjerr ripped off from one of his favorite video games.

As Danjerr runs off blending into the backgrounds, Aren sets off a smoke bomb and starts firing at the surrounding guards outside the duct they were hiding in. Aren is able to pick off a few guards but is gradually getting outnumbered.

Danjerr continues down a brightly lit-up white hallway that leads to some military quarters on the sides and at the end of the very long hall is the destination, the landing docks. The coast is clear until an alarm sounds and dozens of soldiers exit their quarters. Not being seen isn't a problem, but Danjerr still must nimbly maneuver his way through without bumping into someone. Luckily, athleticism and stealth were never a weakness for the confident Danjerr as he leaves the hall and boards the first vessel he sees. The only evidence of his presence is a drop of blood that dropped from his forehead which went unnoticed amidst the chaos.

The entire compound is on full alert. Civilian quarters are locked down. Jaren Lee is walking with Michael Stall to the

USS Avalon and are about to depart for Akyria except the bays are closed. The lock down abruptly ends when soldiers drag a body through the hallway.

"We have the culprit sir, everything else has been locked down and checked. I see no soldier identification, but he bears the Akyrian markings on the temporal region of his head." a soldier comms to Senator Jopalmin.

Jopalmin replies, "Very good soldier. Do one more final check before calling off the lock down. Oh, and one more thing, bring the culprit to me. I have some questions for him."

With the capture, the bays have reopened. Michael immediately fires up the engines of the Avalon. The crew loads up some cargo and equipment. Jaren tries to hurry up and come up with a plan in which to infiltrate Akyria and find an element he knows next to nothing about.

After about an hour into the trip, Jaren's tactician, Miles Sanvado, comes to the bridge of the ship and talks strategy, "Jaren, before we left I managed to get some updated schematics of the Akyrian docking station from our intelligence. Unlike the Akyrians, we won't have to crash our way onto the station. We should be able to dock under diplomacy code as long as they don't detect any of our weaponry. But we must have our weapons deactivated well before our arrival, otherwise they will blast us out of the sky."

Baaaaam!!! The Avalon took a major shift in direction but now seems back on track.

"What the hell?! I know we aren't that close yet. Michael? Is everything alright?......Michael?" Jaren comms to the pilot but there is no response.

"Check the crew, I'm going to check what the blazes just happened." Jaren commands to Miles.

As Jaren enters the cockpit everything seems to be normal but asks Michael to confirm, "Are we still on course for Akyria?"

Michael responds firmly, "Yes, sir."

"So what happened earlier then?" Asks Captain Lee.

"Nothing I just bumped my elbow or my hand on

something...I think." Michael answers.

Jaren kind of shifts his eyes in disbelief and turns around to see a blade right at his throat being held by a man he thinks he recognizes once the cloaking deactivates.

The stranger demands, "You're taking this ship to Akyria, unless you'd like to return home without a voice."

Michael reaches for his photon pistol and interrupts "We are not helping a damn Akyrian. I'd rather go down shooting..."

Jaren cuts him off, "Relax, Michael. I doubt this guy would ever go through with killing us. He doesn't go through with anything. Do you Danjerr?"

Danjerr pauses a bit, grinds his teeth and then turns around Jaren and kicks him to the navigator chair. "Well, if you know who I am then you know I'm not an Akyrian."

Michael inquires, "Then how do you explain your tattoos on your head and the Akyrian markings on your daggers?"

Danjerr mockingly replies, "Don't forget that Akyrian Cruiser I came in on."

Jaren, growing furious responds, "That was you?! You could have killed someone! You're more reckless than when you were in the Academy at the Oyioh Citadel."

Danjerr now insulted exclaims, "Hey! It was your officials who shot us down and caused us to wreck in a civilian area! I didn't exactly care for your welcoming committee either."

Jaren raises his voice again, "You came in on an Akyrian Cruiser! Of course they shot you down! What did you expect? You know we're not gonna let you fly in with that weaponry."

Michael chimes in, "Woah, woah, woah, what? Wait, you know this guy captain?"

"I wish I didn't. He's a traitor to Oyioh. He abandoned us when those damn anarchist Progs attacked the Minsteria sector of Oyioh." answers Jaren.

"Traitor?! Traitor?! Is that a joke, *Captain?* I left to save my family in the Minsteria sector. Something I was unable to do because you bastards arrested me for treason. Treason for what? Saving civilians? The only betrayal I see is that of a friend who stopped me from getting to my family." Danjerr is now fuming as his daggers inch closer to their targets.

Jaren reacts, "We can't make such biased decisions on who we can help. I made the calls and you were supposed to follow them."

"It was quite convenient that you commanded us to save your fiance's neighborhood! Yeah, that's right, I know where she lived and I know why we were setup there." Danjerr fires back.

Jaren replies "You know nothing, we were setting up there for tactical purposes."

"Tactical purposes my ass, I always had better tactics than you and this had nothing to do with tactics. You don't even make your own plans. You run with that Miles Sanvado who botched the Laurynie skirmish. I'm sick of this futile retelling of history. In fact, I have no idea why we don't settle this dispute right now." Danjerr fires back as he shifts the direction of his daggers to Jaren's throat.

BLAST!

Danjerr drops to the floor instantly. Smoke coming from his back and as it fades, there appears Miles.

"Miles, what did you do?" asks Jaren.

"Bailing your ass out. What does it look like? You two looked like you were in trouble. Plus, I disagreed about the whole Laurynie thing."

"I wouldn't call it trouble." Michael adds.

"Stun or kill?" asks Jaren Lee.

"What's the correct answer?" asks Miles.

"Tell me it was on stun. We may actually need this guy to help get us on Akyria." Jaren replies somewhat angrily and yet relieved at the same time.

CHAPTER 3:

DARKER SHADOWS

Away from current public view, a once dominating force

in the U.S. now hides in the dark trying to regain its political

power, lost when the earth was ravaged and humanity moved

space-ward which was in the hands of the military. Slowly, they

have gained control of small sectors on Akyria and Oyioh. Some

are even rumored to be on Veeson. Their leader goes by just one

name: Pariah. A name to serve as a constant reminder to his

followers that they are viewed as outcasts and no longer in

power, something he hopes stirs up his audience and recruits.

The Change for Progress group has already taken over Minsteria after several battles and set up their base of operations there. Oyioh is aware of the Progs' stronghold but they would rather not have a civil war and hope the uprising will quell so they can focus on the growing threat on Ikoss as the Ikossians are building a new space station closer to Oyioh.

The Ikossians are the perfect distraction for the Progs who would rather claim Oyioh for their own. But the Progs are greedy and are trying to attain Akyria as well, resulting in their numbers being thinned out. A tactical error that is slowing their own progress.

A dark, cloaked figure comes from an underground entrance and onto a platform which is in shambles due to the sector's destruction. It's the old town square. The figure is fully covered in dark colors and has a mask on which bears no facial structure, it's the Pariah.

Pariah addresses the crowd in Minsteria, "Brothers and

sisters we must change the oppressive government who will not allow our rights which were valid on earth. We invite all to help our cause and help us regain our power we rightfully own. First, some sectors, then Oyioh, then we'll go to Akyria! And we won't stop there, we will change all of humanity to move on to our change for progress. We'll take back Ikoss which the Alliance greedily sold to our enemies."

The message is clear but not accurate as it was the progressive government who sold Ikoss in order to gather funds for people they owed favors to so they could make it onto the new stations. The voice doesn't sound as clear. It is muffled by the mask and perhaps some sound changing device.

Several large groups applaud loudly. The crowd contains pre-Metal Earth loyalists and illegal citizens who are bitter. There are some doubters and some survivors just trying to blend in so as not to be killed, but their numbers are few as most people are swept up in the propaganda maelstrom. United by their hatred, the audience eats up every word despite not knowing who the Pariah really is. They blindly follow a leader who is an excellent orator which distracts from his radical ideas.

Pariah continues, "My people, we cannot sit idle as the world around us refuses the future. The refusal of the future is the refusal of us!" More cheers interrupt the speech. "I am asking you, brothers and sisters, that you go out and recruit as many followers as you can so that when the day of judgement is at hand, it is our hand that will do the judging!"

Pariah acknowledges the roaring crowd and then hastily returns back inside, almost appearing as though he is late for something.

The crowd is in a frenzy and immediately splits into groups and moves outward from Minsteria and into neighboring sectors of Bremmen and Laurynie. The destruction of anything resembling that of the current government is apparent and even churches aren't safe as many go up in flames. The Progs are bringing their own version of the apocalypse to the citizens of Oyioh.

Meanwhile, at a nearby prison, loyalists to the new American Alliance are questioned with borderline torture techniques to search for any inside info they can get about the President or future president.

A young girl has remained silent throughout, her name is Nikailyn. After questioning and brutal slaps to the face she is returned to her cell where she is thrown to the floor. Blood combined with tears run down her face.

"Why don't you just tell them where he is? You're going to kill yourself." asks a fellow cell mate.

"He won't let that happen." Nikailyn replies.

"How can you be sure?" the prisoner inquires.

"He promised. That promise is what gives me hope. And that hope is what will set us free from these radicals." Nikailyn answers.

"I wish I had your optimism, but I hate to break it to you kid. We ain't leaving anytime soon. The government is refusing to deal with these terrorists." chimes in an old man.

"My brother isn't the government. He hasn't forgotten us." Nikailyn answers with great confidence.

The old man fires back, "Well if he ain't the government, I don't know how he's gonna have the firepower to blast the bastards outta here. You're gonna have to look after yourself in here kid. Ain't no one coming to get us. Our government is thinned out and feuding and Lord knows the politicians on Veeson aren't gonna bother to help us either."

Nikailyn, growing frustrated with the surrounding pessimism, turns away to peer out the barred window as she slowly falls asleep, exhausted from the interrogation.

CHAPTER 4:

BACKDOOR MEETING

In a secret chamber of the Oyioh Citadel a covert meeting is taking place between Senator Jopalmin and Brianna Wynn, an ambassador from Ikoss.

"As I'm sure you're aware, we have a bit of a problem here on Oyioh as some rebel groups are gaining power in some of our sectors and we believe they are getting help from Veeson. Seeing how you and Veeson are at odds with each other, why not a little back-scratching deal where you send us some help to stop the uprising and we'll look the other way on your plans to build another space station between us and Veeson." suggests Jopalmin.

"With all due respect sir, we don't need you to let us build our station. How about you look the other way when we take over Veeson from our new space station." answers Brianna.

"Hahaha, oh my dear Brianna, quit the jokes. You don't think we would actually ever let you take Veeson, do you?"quips Jopalmin.

"You can't even control your own station, senator. How do expect to stop us when you can't stop a much smaller and less intelligent enemy?" responds the ambassador.

Senator Jopalmin answers, "Ikoss would be no match for the American Alliance of Oyioh and Akyria. We would never allow it."

After chuckling a little bit Brianna responds, "Now it's you with the jokes senator. We are well aware of the current divide between your two stations. I don't even think you can

agree with Senator Gellar on whether or not its raining outside.
Now look, we need you, once you've been sworn in as president,
to back us in the reason we're going to build our station and why
we would be going into Veeson, which won't be under the flag of
war...at least not at first. And in return we will rid you of your
annoying Progs."

"We won't bother you moving onto Veeson, but if you
think we're just going to let you waltz in there and start a war,
you're completely delusional." Jopalmin claims.

"I guess we'll have to cross that bridge when we get to it,
won't we senator?" the snide ambassador replies.

"I guess we will, but only after you hold up your end of
the bargain clearing out those damn Progs." the Senator
demands.

"Your request will be handled shortly and swiftly."
Brianna Wynn states.

The two shake hands, a usual symbol of agreement but
not for Jopalmin who views it as another sucker that he has just

used as a pawn in his own game.

Jopalmin's scheme is still a mystery and despite having many contacts he never reveals his plans to anyone. Jopalmin has no ties to the Ikossian government so it is surprising why he would so readily agree to work with them instead of Akyria in order to deal with a small uprising. One man who may be aware of anything is his go to guy, Lieutenant Debo.

The senator reaches to his comm, "Lieutenant Debo, bring me the prisoner from the escaped plane crash. It's time to answer some questions."

"Very well sir." answers Debo.

"Oh, and lieutenant, make sure he's in shape to cooperate with the investigation. We have little time to get the information we need before I meet with Senator Gellar today." Jopalmin requests.

"What about the dead pilot? What would you like with him? Have we gone public with official reports yet?" asks Lieutenant Debo.

"Nothing yet, lieutenant. I will make Gellar aware of the situation when we meet. Well, at least aware of what he needs to be aware of." answers the senator.

Jopalmin then changes into his more formal ceremonial tunic as he is about to be sworn in as the new President of the American Alliance in under an hour. His garments are of a clean white and several silver colored circular emblems on it. The garments deflect the inner motives of the senator.

The new alliance uses an alternating of senators between Akyria and Oyioh to be president every four years. Today marks the day where Oyioh obtains the presidency for the next four years.

CHAPTER 5:

FUEL FOR THOUGHT

Meanwhile, on the USS Avalon, Danjerr has just awakened only to find himself in a cell. There's a tray of food and surprisingly the cell is quite clean and nice. It's another over-expenditure forced on the Oyiohan military by the American congress that was still in effect from pre-Metal Earth. The stainless steel, kevlar, and plastic materials dominate the room which varies from the retro interior of his cruiser.

"Shit." Danjerr mutters as he looks for his belongings.

His daggers are missing, but not his jacket, which has the cloaking technology that is unknown to that of the Oyiohan military. The technology was given to Danjerr personally from Senator Gellar to test out as a guinea pig in exchange for information from his days with the Oyiohan military. It is the only working prototype of its kind.

Jaren enters the room questioning, "Well, there's no real reason to small talk. Why were you on that Akyrian Cruiser coming to Oyioh?"

Danjerr remains silent and, at this point, it doesn't even seem as though he's acknowledging the Captain's presence.

"Look Danjerr, we may be able to help each other out here, but we can't help you unless you're willing to communicate." states Jaren.

Danjerr looks up at Jaren as he sits on the floor leaning against the cot, "You know what, maybe I don't want to be helped. Maybe I just felt like goin' for a ride. It was a great freaking ride until your ruthless senator ordered to have us shot down without warning."

"Us?" Inquires Jaren. "Who else was with you? Why is it you always have to drag others down with you?"

"It's what I do. I wake up every morning, take a swig of my soda and think to myself: Hmmm...who can I take down today? Whose life can I ruin along with mine? God, you make me sick with your arrogant self-righteous talk. You have no idea what's really important. You just sit there and give directions to what suits you best and not what suits the Alliance. You get that from your senator." Danjerr responds again with his trademark delivery of sarcasm.

Jaren sighs before continuing, "Well, my mission is more important than your life right now so I'm not gonna let you compromise it if you get in the way. Now, I will let you in on some info to show that I'm willing to work with you. We are on a reconnaissance mission to find an element that will solve our fuel shortage problems. We're not sure who has it, but if Ikoss beats us to the recovery, they will horde it for themselves and corner the market giving them extreme economical power. That's something we can't afford to have with them already advancing their aggressive growing military as well. So, after hearing that, what do you wanna do? I know you are best buds with the Akyrian senator. What has he told you?" There is a pause in the conversation before Jaren continues, "You must know something. Our intelligence suggests Akyria has the Zionium."

"Zionium? Is that what they're calling it? Well, then you know more about it than I do." Says Danjerr.

Jaren follows, "You may know more than you think you do. We'll still need you to get onto Akyria too. So, what do you say?"

There's another long pause between the two and then Danjerr turns his head but Jaren responds by pacing to the left to get back in view.

"Payment." Danjerr mutters.

"Excuse me?" Jaren disgustedly asks.

Danjerr immediately answers, "Payment. Payment. What's gonna be my motivation to helping a person who let my family die? And I'm not talking dollars."

"Forget it!" yells Jaren.

"I can't forget it! Or forgive it. You really don't care what you did to me, do you? I mean, if my family died, but I was able to get there and help others I could maybe live with it, but I couldn't. You guys wouldn't even give me a chance. You have no idea what it feels like to have your family die knowing you couldn't do a damn thing about it!" Danjerr thunders back.

"Fine. Make your demands. But we can only deliver appropriate requests." replies a frustrated Jaren.

Danjerr leans back, "Me and Aren will need a new vessel..."

Jaren interrupts, "You brought Aren into this? Where is he? Oh shit, he didn't make it, did he? He was your pilot wasn't he? Damn it Danjerr, you're ruining people's lives with your..."

"Shut the hell up! Listen up, I got a dose of some truth for ya. Aren made it out of the wreck with me, that's a fact. I have no idea about our mercenary pilot or my recon drone. Now, I'm guessing the person with the info we need on Aren and MZX is your best pal, Senator Jopalmin." says Danjerr.

Jaren quickly asks, "MZX?"

To which Danjerr responds, "That was my recon drone, try to keep up here."

Miles enters the holding area and, thankfully for everyone involved, becomes an excuse for the heated debate to end.

"Miles, keep an eye on him, I'm going back to the bridge to see how close we are to Akyria." demands Jaren.

"Sir." Miles reacts along with a salute.

Jaren makes his way to the Comm Room to contact Janah. He doesn't worry about troubling Jopalmin about the news of capturing Danjerr. The screen after several rings turns on with Janah overjoyed and yet somewhat upset it took Jaren so long to call. "Janah, Sorry about the delay, we had an unexpected meet-up with an "old friend."

"You better be sorry." Janah sarcastically responds before she finishes, "Anyway, who did you come across?"

"It's Danjerr. I know I should report to Jopalmin about this, but I was thinking about how you don't trust the senator."

"I don't exactly trust Danjerr, either." Janah interrupts.

"Well, I know that, but with the Senator shooting down an ally cruiser without warning and then not releasing any details, I'm just not sure what he'd do to Danjerr. I mean, I know Danjerr and we've had our differences, but I don't think he deserves what Jopalmin would probably do to him." says Jaren.

Janah responds, "You're probably right about the senator, but you still have to be careful. Danjerr has betrayed Oyioh dozens of times over. He works for himself, not the Alliance." Janah pauses before finishing, "Jaren, I.....I need you to come back. That's all. Your family needs you and I won't stand for that traitor to screw it all up!"

"Don't worry, Janah. Remember, I got Miles and Michael and the rest of the crew to watch after him. Hopefully, this trip won't be as difficult as Jopalmin thinks it might be. Look, Janah, I gotta get back on task so I can get to you as soon as possible. "

"I guess your right." Janah sighs and finishes, "I love you."

"I love you too, and I'll be back ASAP. I promise." Jaren says and then presses the button to deactivate the link-up.

Back at the holding cells, Miles walks over to Danjerr's food tray and pauses. Then he asks, "Is it true that you dragged Aren into this?"

Danjerr answers, "I didn't drag anyone. Anyone who comes with me, comes with me because they choose to. Did you guys ever think that people may agree with me and we're on a common mission. Seriously."

Clank! Miles kicks over the tray in frustration. "I don't know how much the Akyrians are paying you to backstab Oyioh, but if you try anything that endangers any of our crew..." Miles draws his pulse pistol, commonly referred to as the Stiletto, and points it at Danjerr's head. "Well, you just better not do anything stupid. There's no doubt that I'll make you regret it."

Amused at the threat, Danjerr busts out with a loud laugh totally mocking Miles. Embarrassed, Miles hits Danjerr over the head with the butt of his Stiletto.

"Meet Stiletto." Miles says as he looks at his pulse gun. "Way more effective than these archaic weapons you lug around." Miles has now turned his attention to the confiscated Akyrian daggers of Danjerr. After a bit of a pause Miles finishes his thought, "I wonder...how many lives have you claimed with these primitive blades?"

Danjerr answers, "None. At least none that I know of. Let's put it this way, they've put down less than your Stiletto."

"I find that hard to believe. I've heard your stories and read your reports. It's a mess." replies Miles.

"Take another look at those daggers. Not all the markings are Akyrian. Some of them are Aramaic, some Roman, and some of European descent. The blades are artifacts from the

Crusades." Danjerr informs Miles.

"Oh come on, you expect me to believe that you somehow stumbled upon relics of the Crusades?" replies Miles.

"No, I expect you to assume I'm a liar like your higher-ups have always told you. I received these blades from an old friend, a priest, Kellen Hopkins. He blessed them one last time before he died and gave them to me. The legend of these blades is that they've never taken a life as long as the blood from a previous battle was cleansed with holy water. So, like I said, they've never killed."

"That you know of." fires back Miles. "I know you'd like me to believe that tale so maybe we let you go and you can continue on your personal war for freedom or vengeance, whatever reason is convenient for you."

"Has it never occurred to you that the media are liars and will say anything to serve their agenda? An agenda I don't factor into." questions Danjerr.

After a pause, Miles asks, "So *have* these daggers been

cleansed since the last battle?"

"No. I, unfortunately, had to incapacitate a few guards to get our cruiser and then to escape the wreckage. And no, I don't have any holy water on me, the container easily got destroyed in the crash." Answers Danjerr.

At that very moment Jaren comes in with a commanding strut, "Don't believe a word he says Miles. He can be quite manipulative. Isn't that right, Mr. Councilman of Strategic Defenses?"

Danjerr sarcastically laughs and replies, "Oh, you heard about that one, huh? You shouldn't blame me for the gullible fallacies of others."

"Forget the jokes. It's time for business. We are about to pull into the docking bay at Akyria, and you're going to help us out. We need the codes to dock in your military installation. I've already briefed you on why we're here. However, we need to know who to talk to in order to see what we can find out about the element. Intel points to Akyria, let's hope they are correct. If it was an Ikossian ship on the excavation, then we may already be to late. We've already went over the possible repercussions of that scenario." Jaren says with authority.

Danjerr thinks for a second and then responds, "Look, I don't know as much as you like to think. However, I will help you out in exchange for releasing Aren, MZX-20, and a new ship. Having said all that, I'm not leaving this ship without my daggers."

"Deal, but you don't touch the daggers until we step foot on Akyria." answers Jaren. "And remember, there's more to this than us. If we fail and don't obtain the element, and it falls into the wrong hands, then you can forget about the American Alliance's ability to stay together."

"Your flair for the dramatic is noted. Don't worry, I'll be a team player." quips Danjerr.

CHAPTER 6:

INAUGURATION

Jopalmin makes his way out of the Oyioh Citadel and into

the Town Greens. He raises his arms after hearing a grand

applause. Several burly armor-clad service guards escort him to

the podium where Senator Gellar reluctantly awaits to pass off

his power to Jopalmin.

The Greens are exotically decorated with some rare

flowers that have trouble staying alive in the new artificial lighting greenhouses that exist on Veeson. White and silver

banners engulf the balconies that overhang the government

buildings in the district. Thousands are eagerly awaiting

Jopalmin's speech as many are expecting him to discuss a new

plan to strengthen the American Alliance in regards to the fast

growing Ikossian fleet.

Senator Gellar makes his way to the podium to give his

final address as President. "Citizens and patriots of Oyioh and

Akyria, today marks a new era of the American Alliance in

which I will pass off my power to my fellow countryman,

Senator Jopalmin. We have been through many struggles to

return life to normalcy that once existed on earth. We are getting

closer to that dream. We have made great strides since our first

"Metal Earth" president. And as I have improved upon former

President Brock's success, it is my hope and belief that Senator

Jopalmin will improve upon my administration."

Before Gellar continues his speech he is interrupted by a

loud applause. Some heckling, however, can be overheard in

some areas.

"Thank you all! It is this kind of enthusiasm and energy that we will need to make sure we succeed in stopping all evil and terror that wants to try and destroy this new life we have created. We will not, we must not ever let this happen! We must come together united to defeat them!"

Gellar is interrupted by another thunderous applause.

"Ladies and gentlemen, the man who will help us succeed, your new president, Mr. Maurice Jopalmin!"

The crowd is now in a frenzy as Jopalmin takes the stage and shakes hands with Senator Gellar. Jopalmin, attempts to quiet the crowd so he can begin his speech, but the crowd is relentless.

Men, women, and children of all races are on their feet, but then without notice a large group of people in the audience reveal themselves in dark colored robes and draw weapons ranging from knives to Stilettos and other various photon pistols. Gellar's guards take notice and step out in front of Gellar.

The once excited crowd is now filled with fear and are in a panic as cries for help go unnoticed and the terrorists begin slaughtering innocents. Only a few of the terrorists use the guns, everything is mostly done by knives and other small easy to hide weaponry. Gellar's best guards now surround him and guide him to the nearest government vehicle, but none are close enough before he gets cutoff by some terrorists. The guards, led by Lieutenant Debo, quickly gun them down but the number of them are overwhelming and they quickly lose track of their flanks.

BLAST!

A loud gunshot from a foreign photon rifle alarms the guards to turn around and see Jopalmin lying face first on the metallic floor now drenched in a blood trail leading from the President's neck.

Debo takes the remaining guards with Senator Gellar and retreat back to the Citadel and fortify it from any attacks. Senator Gellar begins to interrogate all guards about any information they know of the enemy. "Debo, call in some reinforcements.

Everybody else, anybody at all, know who or what that was about? Who had it in for Jopalmin? Get me names and any other connections or contacts you can find."

"I think there's your answer, sir." Debo says after hearing an Ikossian Dreadnought hover in as the crew of black-clothed terrorists make their escape before the Oyiohan army can make it to the Greens.

"That's a bold move by the Ikossians to assassinate him on Oyioh where the Alliance military is located. I just can't believe it." says Gellar.

"With all due respect sir, maybe that's why they made the move. We wouldn't expect it. None of us did. It caught us off guard. I guess it was just something we took for granted." Debo replies.

After a pause, Gellar sighs and states, "Damn it. We did take it for granted. We must make sure this situation stays under control and we don't let the public go nuts. I need someone in charge of helping any survivors in the Greens. I also need someone to let me in on all info Jopalmin had available. And, for our future's sake, limit all media until we get things straightened out."

"That's classified sir." States the lieutenant.

"Not anymore." Gellar fires back angrily. "I'm in charge now and we need to work together like we should have before. We must make sure no one's lives die in vain. Jopalmin and I may have had our differences but we're still all part of the Alliance. Now, the info I requested. All of it, now! And someone patch me through to Veeson."

Another guard comes out of the back, "Senator Gellar. I know someone who may know something about what's going on."

"Bring him in immediately." Gellar demands.

A beat up man in black and blue attire that is now visibly torn walks out with his hands cuffed behind him. His head droops with exhaustion. Suddenly he looks up.

"Aren?!" Senator Gellar shouts. "My God, what's going

on here. What happened to you?!"

Aren coughs and faintly says, "Why don't you ask our allies? They still have a voice."

Gellar turns his attention to the Lieutenant Debo who replies, "Sir, we don't know anything. Honestly! We have our orders from Jopalmin and that's it. None of us ever know his plans, his meetings, or what went on when he requested Aren's appearance."

"Why is he in cuffs?! He's with the Alliance!" Gellar exclaims.

"Trespassing sir. He was traveling in an Akyrian Cruiser with a couple accomplices over restricted Oyioh space. Jopalmin ordered that we shoot it down immediately. The pilot is dead and there was a busted reconnaissance drone, model MZX-20. Aren claims he was the only one who survived the crash, but Jopalmin insisted there was another, but we never came up with anything, just spices, food, and some general goods. However, it's not our fault Akyria was using a cruiser as a freighter." answers Debo.

Senator Gellar recognizes the drone and immediately realizes Danjerr Ohm is the other survivor, but bites his tongue on revealing his name as he trusts Danjerr to accomplish anything and do so for the good of the Alliance.

Gellar addresses Aren, "Aren, what did Jopalmin question you about? Why would the Ikossians want to off him? Anything you know, the smallest tidbit would be a huge help."

Aren replies, "He was obsessed with something he only referred to as 'the element.' I think he was referring to the alternative fuel source you wanted us to investigate. To be honest, I'm not sure anyone has it. Regardless, Jopalmin believed the element consists of some new unknown metal, chemical, or whatever from the meteors that hit. I guess the toxic gasses must have cleared up enough that someone can get to the impact crater and try to recover some. But the funny thing is, Jopalmin never talked about it as a fuel source like we did. It seemed as though he wanted to use it as a weapon to take back Ikoss from the Russians. (Cough, cough!) He insisted we knew something more about it when all we were doing was doing a routine intel check as to whether or not the element was fact or fiction."

"But how did the Ikossians know about the element when it was apparently an Alliance fleet that made the discovery?" asks Gellar.

"Same way we do, sir. Double agents, spies, wiretapping, and advanced satellite cameras. However, here's the confusing part. One night, I peered though the beautiful view-window in my cell and noticed a diplomat or ambassador with Ikossian markings leave the premises. It seems strange to me that the Ikossians would off Jopalmin if he had been working with them." answers Aren.

Gellar continues, "Intriguing news indeed. Someone get Aren to the med-bay and cleaned up. I want him ready to go with me back to Akyria. Forget the patch through to Veeson. Have them meet me at my office on Akyria where things will be safe. Have the army and any capable civilian help clean and aid the victims and secure this station from any future attack."

"A vessel will be ready for you travel in about two hours Senator." says Lieutenant Debo.

"You better get it to me in 20 minutes!" Gellar shouts as he leaves to prepare for his trip.

CHAPTER 7:

DIVISION.....AND MATH

The crew of the USS Avalon exits the landing dock and into the civilian quarters. With Danjerr leading the way, none of the Akyrian guards or mercenaries even question the accompaniment of some Oyiohan soldiers.

Jaren wastes no time giving orders, "Miles, go with Danjerr to meet his contacts. I'll meet up with you guys in one hour at the Akyrian embassy. Michael, I need you to stay here with the rest of the crew to secure this sector and ensure the Avalon is ready in case we need to bail out in a hurry."

"And you will be where?" Danjerr asks with a bit of an attitude.

"I need to check in with someone." Answers Jaren.

"Jopalmin? I swear if you set me up Jaren, my daggers will claim their first kill." replies Danjerr.

"Sheath your weapons. No, not Jopalmin." says Jaren.

Danjerr figures out who, "Oh, gee, so once again as you bark orders to everyone else to do dirty work, you go and talk to your girlfriend. Unbelievable. Let's go Miles, if you're coming along. I don't have time for this crap."

Jaren, angles his eyes with a disgusted look as Danjerr takes off in a hurry with Miles lagging behind. Jaren looks around and signals to Michael that he's taking off.

The light is starting to fade as Akyria's revolution around the earth is starting to block it. Lights are illuminating the modern sector of Faseelle, the largest sector on Akyria that serves as the capital. Jaren makes his way to the Akyrian Embassy where he finds a comm room. Jaren dials and the comm rings but there's no answer and it follows through to the voice-mail.

"Janah, Janah? Hey, if you're screening your calls, pick up, it's me, Jaren. Well, I was just checking in letting you know I'm on Akyria at the embassy."

Suddenly a nearby door opens revealing Janah who rushes over to Jaren and gives an enthusiastic hug. "Jaren, I saw the Avalon come in. Oh am I glad to see you. Have you talked to anyone yet?"

Jaren replies, "What do you mean?"

"You haven't heard?! How have you not heard about the assassination?!" Janah frantically asks.

"Assassination?!" Jaren shockingly responds.

"The Ikossians assassinated President Jopalmin at his inauguration speech. A giant mass of black hooded terrorists seemingly came out of nowhere and then left in an Ikossian Dreadnought before the Oyiohan military could arrive." Janah answers.

"Why didn't you comm me when this happened?" asks Jaren.

Janah answers while some tears start to fall from her face, "I panicked. There was chaos everywhere in the sector. I took the first shuttle to get to the embassy at Faseelle. Word has it that Senator Gellar is gonna remain president until this problem gets sorted out. He's supposed to talk to the presidents of Veeson and Ikoss."

"Do you know when this is supposed to happen?" asks Jaren.

At this moment, on the televisions in the embassy, the channel switches to the news conference of the Ikoss ambassador speaking, its' Brianna Wynn. The conference is taking place on her vessel, another Dreadnought on its way to Akyria.

Wynn is already in mid-sentence when the channel switched over to it and now draws the attention of Jaren Lee and Janah Omen.

"Make no mistake about it, the Ikossians were not involved. We are investigating into the ship used to transport the terrorists. We will have more information later when we meet at the Akyrian embassy." States Brianna Wynn.

Ambassador Wynn refuses to take any questions over the comm link and immediately shuts it off. Jaren looks stunned as everything still seems quite surreal.

"Looks like we'll just stay here and wait for everyone to come to us." Jaren states.

Meanwhile, Danjerr and Miles have made it to a VIP room at The Celestial night club awaiting Danjerr's contact. The lights are flashing and the sounds are bumping. Miles excuses himself from the table, "I need to get some air. These lights are killing me. I'll be back in five."

No one has arrived yet. Danjerr looks around for a clock as he is growing impatient and hates the establishment. Sweat starts to slide down his face as the place is boiling inside from the amount of people in the club, as well as the fact that his contact who is always timely hasn't arrived yet is making him a bit nervous. Danjerr wipes the sweat away with his index finger.

Right as Danjerr begins to lean back on his chair he hears a loud groan from the exit where Miles went. Several feet can be heard making their way towards the door. Danjerr, stunned but always thinking, quickly activates his Cloak of Shadows. However, the multiple strobes and many colors of lights are slightly altering its effectiveness so Danjerr makes a dash to get underneath the table.

The door is violently kicked in and a half dozen of black clothed men come in and scare off any civilian in sight. A couple seconds later, a black-hooded figure walks in, it's the Pariah.

Pariah delivers orders, "Find the mercenary. Alive. And destroy the place. It reeks of the old ways we must abolish. If he won't come willingly, bribe him with our bait. The girl will finally prove her worth."

After the terrorists make their way through the club, Danjerr sneaks out the exit and finds Miles. He reaches to try and find a pulse. There isn't one. Danjerr finds a small vent outside to sneak into and comms Jaren.

"Jaren, can you hear me. What happened to you meeting up with us?"

Jaren responds, "My plans changed. Jopalmin has been assassinated by the Ikossians. Gellar is supposed to be at the embassy any minute now and I'm gonna get answers."

"Why didn't you comm me before. We could've bailed and maybe your crew member wouldn't have met his maker earlier than he should have. We got jumped by some black hooded terrorists while waiting for our contact." Danjerr says.

"What?! Does anyone with you stay alive? I don't think you could've saved your family even if you got to them the way you protect people. First your hijacked pilot, then Aren gets captured, and now Miles. That's a lot of guilt you must live with." Jaren is again pissed off with Danjerr's ability to lead.

"Bold words for someone who is always just going to some safe confines with his girlfriend when the rest of us do the work that requires our hands to get dirty. Sometimes they get bloody, not by choice. You know what, I'm not even gonna follow your plan. You never follow it, but expect everyone else to and we are the ones who suffer for it. Send Gellar my regards, but I'm gonna settle this conflict the old fashioned way before politics get involved and screw everything up." Danjerr whispers angrily and shuts off his comm.

Danjerr leans back his head against the rusty inside of the vent pondering what Jaren said. The body count is getting too high for anyone to be comfortable and so far the math of good minus evil isn't equaling victory.

Danjerr looks at his Akyrian daggers and notices the blood on them have dried. He knows he doesn't have time to find holy water to clean them. The upcoming battle of good and evil is going to require him to try and incapacitate the terrorists without fatal wounds. A fact that seems to be more and more trivial considering what the terrorists have done, but Danjerr shifts his head and realizes he must not drop to their standards.

CHAPTER 8:
DON'T FORGET
ABOUT VEESON

Senator Gellar's vessel has finally arrived on Akyria and

he makes his way toward the Citadel. Lieutenant Debo follows

shortly behind with a couple of guards. The looks in the guards'

eyes display a bit of nervousness as they walk by a couple of the

Akyrian mercenaries. One mercenary, dressed in some old tan

fatigues and a pure silver Titan mark IV body armor which is the

latest armor of the Oyiohan army. It is also only made and

handed out to Oyiohan soldiers. The armor is scuffed and scratched in multiple places and riddled with blaster rifle shots.

The group finally arrives at a grand entrance with top of the line security. Gellar places his hand in tray filled with a green, solid gel-like substance that reads his DNA. Upon passing it, large stainless steel doors open sideways into the walls. The group passes through the entrance which is lined with a red laser-like barrier that scans the group, the doors shut behind them once the lasers detects a foreign weapon.

"Remain still and await security or suffer the consequences." states an automated recording.

Gellar looks back at Lieutenant Debo.

"Sorry, sir. I forgot I picked it up after the skirmish on Oyioh." Says Debo.

Gellar shakes his head and responds, "System override, code 4-3-1."

"Voice and code input accepted. Override enabled. Have a good day senator." Answers the automated security.

The entrance to the back of the embassy leads immediately to Gellar's office so the crew won't have to deal with any civilians and keep a low profile. The lavish roman-looking office is just as Gellar left it for his trip to Oyioh except one thing.

It's Captain Jaren Lee who demands, "I need answers."

"You're in my office, soldier. I'll get my answers first. And I'll take my seat back, thank you." Gellar kicks Jaren out of the seat and relaxes in the nice leather chair built like a throne.

"So what answers do you request senator?" asks Jaren.

"I need to know anything you know about the Ikossians and their affiliation with Jopalmin. Aren, *one* of *your* prisoners saw an Ikossian diplomat leave Jopalmin's office?"

"Aren, Aren's alright? Where is he?" Jaren demandingly asks.

"He's in the med-bay, he'll be fine. Back on task. What do you know?"

Jaren responds, "I don't know about any of Jopalmin's

contacts. I tried to stay out that stuff. Guess I always figured I

didn't want to know any of that backdoor politics bull shit."

"Fair enough, captain. What about the element? Were

you guys able to recover any trace amount of it?" asks the

senator.

"No, we were under the command to retrieve it from you

when we were ambushed by *your* mercenary. We never even

went down to earth to extract something. Our intelligence

reported Akyria was already in possession of some. Jopalmin

sent me on a recon mission to see if it was true and to see what

your intentions were. So, no. The answer is no, we don't have

anything. We don't even know if the Ikossians have any either,

but we definitely can't deny their desire for some." answers

Jaren.

Gellar reacts, "That's true, however, that seems a little

rash, even for the Ikossians. So, you said you ran into Danjerr.

What did you do with him? He may be of more help. Especially

considering we have nothing right now, including the fact that no one knows anything about the Zionium other than that the other guy has it."

Before Jaren even has a chance to answer, he is interrupted by the video comm-link turning on with Veeson's Prime Minister Hinkle getting ready to address Gellar.

"Gellar. We have tried to contact the Ikossians, however, we are getting mixed answers. Reports from Ambassador Wynn states no involvement in the assassination, but they have no comment on the use of what is obviously an Ikossian Dreadnought ship. Ikossian news reports are even stating that some far-left reactionaries may be organized in an underground movement. Although that is purely speculation at this point."

Gellar replies, "Damn it. Those socialists aren't gonna cooperate with us. They never do. Alright Hinkle, I'll get back to you when we figure out more. Hopefully I can get through to Ikoss' president and get some answers."

Senator Gellar closes the video comm-link while muttering, "Useless then, useless now."

"What do you suggest we do next, sir?" asks Lieutenant Debo.

Jaren jumps to answer for Gellar, "We need to figure out if the attacks are constrained to Oyioh or if they're planning an attack on Akyria as well. How many soldiers or mercenaries can you spare, senator? Most of the Oyiohan military is cleaning up the massacre at the Greens."

"Not many, I have a couple personal guards that are here with us. We have several mercenaries, but I can't be sure as to who is where. They work for many employers. They very may well be off this station entirely." answers Gellar.

Lieutenant Debo asks, "Is there any chance they're working for the Ikossians and are betraying you? A little two-for-one deal. They get paid to take out our good soldiers that they hate."

"No chance at all. I pay them quite well for their loyalties. I allow them to work for anyone else as long as they don't challenge the ability of the Akyrian government to operate.

If they do, it wouldn't be hard to find another mercenary to take him out. None of the mercs I hire are that dumb." Gellar replies.

"I'll try to shuttle some more soldiers here if we can spare any, but it could be several hours before they can even arrive." Jaren adds.

"Sounds good. Jaren, why don't you secure the civilian portion of the embassy. Debo, secure the rear perimeter and surveillance. I'll let ya know when I get in contact with Ambassador Wynn." Gellar states.

The soldiers make their appropriate paths, but Jaren makes his way to Janah. Although it's only a couple rooms down from the civilian entrance to the embassy.

"It's about time, so what did you find out?" asks Janah.

Not quite the welcoming Jaren was expecting, he replies, "You must go home. It's gonna be in our best interest to clear out civilians in case their next plan of attack is on Senator Gellar. It may not be safe here."

"It may not be safe out there. At least in here, there are a few guards and two or three mercenaries loyal to the senator." Janah fires back.

"Janah, please. Heed my advice." demands Jaren.

"Look, you're in here, I'll be safe. Besides, Danjerr isn't here. He's out there. That's probably where the danger will be. He finds the trouble. Maybe you guys should look for him, he'll lead ya to the enemy in a heartbeat." states Janah.

Jaren sighs and responds, "Tried. His comms are off, and he's not answering back after our last conversation. I believe he's already found the trouble."

"I knew it. Just promise me you won't let him get in the way. He could put all of our lives in danger. I don't like thinking about us being separated because of his reckless ways." Janah replies.

Jaren grabs Janah by the hand and leans his forehead against hers and says, "I promise. You will never have to worry about us being separated. Ever. We're gonna solve this problem, no matter the threat. And when it's all said and done, we'll take the next three months off together."

Janah jokes back, "Let's see how bad this goes, it may have to be 6 months."

The two share a small laugh. An embrace follows before Jaren reaches into his pocket and gets on one knee. He pulls out a smooth silver little box. Janah's face becomes flushed with tears.

Jaren opens the box, reaches it out towards Janah revealing the beautiful ring and says, "I promise to make it through this. Do you promise to make it through with me?"

Janah rushes her hands in front of her face as tears roll off the side of her cheeks and pauses before she has the voice to say, "Yes, yes. I promise."

Jaren gets off his knee and hugs Janah tighter than he's ever hugged her before. After the two release, Jaren walks away saying, "Lock the door behind me. We'll be back in this moment before you know it."

Janah, still somewhat speechless, nods her head while

wiping away the tears and then locks the door. Jaren rejoins the

couple of soldiers and clears out the civilian quarters.

CHAPTER 9:

TO STALK A HUNTER

Danjerr notices his comm has incoming messages from

Jaren but is ignoring them. His comm battery has limited life left

anyway. It was damaged when he dove under the table to

conceal himself from the attack at the club. Danjerr notices his

scar on his forehead from the cruiser crash has reopened. The

darkness of the vent makes it hard to find some gauze in his

jacket. The scar is so close to his eye it is impossible to wrap the gauze around his head without blocking his vision so Danjerr just holds pressure to it for awhile and dabs it until the bleeding has ceased.

Danjerr thinks back to himself, "I wonder what that black veiled terrorist was talking about. Were they looking for me or Miles? Couldn't be me, I don't have any affiliation with Jopalmin. But what about the girl? Miles has no living female relatives alive."

Danjerr pauses for a bit and then perks up as an unsuspected thought has hit him, "No! It can't be....Nikailyn! Those terrorists weren't Ikossian! Those radical bastards! "

Danjerr gathers his things and takes some adrenaline stimulants. Time is not a luxury and if Nikailyn is still alive, he wants to waste as little time as possible finding his sister. He sheaths his daggers and makes his back through the club. There are a few remaining terrorists destroying the place and confiscating documents.

A door opens. The terrorists turn to see no one coming

through. They totally dismiss it believing they left no survivors.

As they all turn their attention back to what they were doing, SLASH! A body drops, his knee tendons slashed like ribbons.

SLASH! Another victim.

SLASH! SLASH! Two more drop, both holding their sides as they fall in agony. All of their weapons scattered as they squirm on the floor gasping for air. One terrorists lies at the door with no clue what has hit his men. He shakes nervously, barely able to even hold onto his Stiletto. He starts pointing it randomly and firing until the rounds have run out.

All of the sudden a voice shouts, "It's scary not knowing when death is at your door and you have no chance to help yourself, or those around you."

The terrorists asks, "What do you want? I can pay you!"

The voice now comes from a different spot of the room, "I want you to feel what you made these people feel when you came in and murdered them. I want you to face the terror you made Minsteria feel, my family feel, my friends feel."

"Please, please! I'll stop. I promise. I can help you, I'll tell you whatever you want just let me go. I got a family." pleads the terrorists.

The voice again jumps to a different spot, "Funny, I don't recall you giving a crap about anyone else's family. Why should I care about yours? However, I can use some information."

"Anything, ask anything." States the terrorists who is now soaking from tears and a nervous sweat.

"I need a couple things: the location of your prisoners, where's your leader and where's he going?" the voice says as it is getting closer.

"Prisoners? What prisoners? The Ikossians don't take prisoners." Claims the terrorist before he is then immediately kicked to the ground for his lie.

"Don't feed me the Ikossian bull shit. I've seen the weapons from all you, you're carrying Stilettos, not Roulettes or Peacekeepers. You all have Alliance weaponry. I know you aren't the Ikossians. I don't care how you raided an Ikossian Dreadnought. Answer my questions murderer!" demands the voice.

The terrorist gathers himself and gets back to his feet, "Alright, alright, alright. The prisoners are on board the Dreadnought."

"And your leader, where's he running to, who's his target?" asks the voice.

"Not he. She. She plans to attack the embassy. Something about taking down the president and the president-to-be would create enough havoc and anarchy where she could swoop in and fill the void and take control. Can I go now? Please." responds the terrorist.

"Too many people were killed by your hand. You don't get to walk away." says the voice.

The terrorist covers his head fearing death, but as he reaches high he feels a searing pain. His Achilles tendons have both been shredded and he begins to stumble in place trying to maintain his balance.

The voice, now in front of the terrorist, begins talking as the voice is slowly revealed to be Danjerr when he deactivates his cloaking armor.

"Good night!" Danjerr says as he kicks the terrorist in the chest and to the floor. The terrorist is all but helpless with his ankles out of commission.

Danjerr has now become fully visible and closes the conversation, "I'm not gonna kill you. There are things for worse than death. And I don't think the people who will find you squirming here will be as lenient as I was."

The attack was swift and thorough, but most importantly to Danjerr, without mortal casualty. The information will prove vital as he is alone now. Although it isn't the fact that he'll be on his own that will be the hardest decision. He must decide what he will do first. Will he make his way to the embassy to help protect Gellar and prevent the last attack by the terrorists or will he go and rescue the prisoners which may or may not include his sister? However, Danjerr is well aware of how it'll look if he leaves for family again and drifts from the main mission.

Another fact not lost on Danjerr is the way he's chastised Jaren for always being selfish and worrying about his fiancé over the mission and well being of others. Hypocrites and the lack of a moral compass in others have driven him to become bitter and he has strived to never be like the heathens who ruin the American way of life. However, the choices before were never as difficult as this situation, it has been three years since he's seen his sister.

A look of certainty has now come to Danjerr's face, brows angled, eyes focused, grip tight. He wipes the blades clean on a banner outside the side entrance of the club. Clean, but still not pure, the blades have still not been cleansed by holy water.

Sirens sound and Danjerr notices blue and red lights flashing around the corner, he doesn't have time for questioning. He activates the cloaking and makes his way out of the scene with ease. The mission is clear.

CHAPTER 10:
WHO'S WHO?

The Akyrian embassy has been emptied of any civilian presence. The guards and mercenaries believe they will be prepared for the futile but imminent attack by whoever assassinated President Jopalmin.

However, their numbers are few. A count of four personal bodyguards for Gellar reside with him in his office in the rear of the embassy. Captain Jaren Lee sits in the lobby with two guards who worked under Jopalmin. Lieutenant Debo awaits the back entrance with the mercenary in Oyiohan-clad armor. Only a handful of mercenaries are out patrolling the streets of Akyria. Michael Stall and what's left of the crew sit at the USS Avalon.

In all, only about 20 men are in position for the assault and the reinforcements from Oyioh won't arrive for another two hours. The amount of those soldiers coming aren't known as many stayed behind to secure Oyioh and help its victims recover from the previous attack.

There's a knock at the rear. The visitor is guised in a black veil with followers to her left and right, about a dozen dressed in the same black robes worn by the terrorists. About another two dozen line all the way back to an Ikossian Dreadnought. The Pariah and the anarchist movement followers of the Change for Progress have arrived for the last kill.

Two mercenaries spot the black-clad mob and open fire on the terrorists. The Pariah stands patiently unshaken by the gunfire and relies on the followers to return fire.

A nervous henchman asks, "Pariah, what if he's not here? We'll all get gunned down in about ten minutes once the soldiers know our location. We should've brought more men!"

The Pariah looks over at the disgruntled henchman, "Lack of confidence? Not a quality I need in a servant."

BLAST!

The Pariah guns down the terrorist as a message to the other followers who question the judgement of the movement's leader.

The rear entrance inexplicably opens and the Pariah and about 14 surviving terrorists enter and the door locks behind them leaving the two mercenaries outside, both badly wounded.

"Lieutenant." says the Pariah.

Lieutenant Debo salutes and then comms to Senator Gellar, "Senator, Ambassador Wynn is here to see you."

The senator responds, "Send her in lieutenant."

Debo leads the terrorists through the embassy which is lacking life allowing the militants to easily setup for a takeover.

The move has been quiet and stealth thanks to the betrayal of Lieutenant Debo, who incapacitated his partnered mercenary. With the mercenary out of the way, Debo took out the surveillance once he found out the Pariah had arrived.

Debo leads the Pariah to the entrance of Gellar's grand office, a room which is comparable in size to a small auditorium. Debo walks in first by himself and walks behind everyone and leans on Gellar's desk.

"Where is she?" asks the senator.

"I'm right here." the Pariah answers as she walks in.

Gellar's bodyguards raise their Stiletto's at the Pariah.

"I wouldn't do that gentlemen." Debo suggests as he has now taken aim at Senator Gellar.

"Debo, what are you doing?!" asks Gellar.

"About to make a change for progress." claims Debo.

"Have you lost it?! This movement will never succeed. Don't you know you all will be hunted down for this?" Gellar states as he rubs his wrist triggering an alarm on his watch to alert any nearby ally, but the alarms have been deactivated by Debo.

Six of Pariah's thugs walk in surrounding the room. As the terrorists march in, the Pariah removes the veil. And speaks with her true voice, "Does my voice sound more familiar senator?"

"Ambassador Wynn? What, what? You don't know what you're doing. Double crossing the Ikossians and now you have the audacity to assassinate an American President. You think you'll just walk out of here unattested?" says Gellar.

"Go ahead Senator, ask me what I want, ask me." Brianna Wynn says. She then raises her gun and yells, "Ask me!"

Gellar struggles to say it, "What do you want?"

"I want a new America. The America that those meteors destroyed. The life we had. I do *not* want the old American life your government has reverted us back to. We need a leader who will bring us back to the socialist utopia we once attained to perfection!" states Brianna Wynn.

"Utopia?! Utopia, Brianna? You're joking, right? America had it's highest death rate in it's history. The place was in shambles with ridiculously high taxes and the people seeing none of that money coming back to them. It was only a utopia for the politicians in power." Gellar responds.

Brianna looks over to her guards who respond with immediate fire on Gellar's bodyguards. Gellar is now alone and unarmed against the threat.

About fifty yards down, Jaren whips his head in the direction of the office and says to his two soldiers, "Gunfire, come on let's go."

Little does Jaren know they are about to run into a dozen terrorists before even reaching Gellar's office. More unfortunate is that terrorists have now taken full operation of the surveillance Debo rigged and know the location of Jaren and his men, not to mention Janah. The terrorists have moved from their holding positions and move out in an aggressive assault on what they see as intruders.

Jaren grabs his comm, "Michael, get down here now. Forget the Avalon. We may have problems here. We heard gunfire from the rear of the embassy. We're making our way to the back ASAP."

"Roger that, we'll be there in five. Word from Oyioh is that backup will arrive in a half hour with about 50 troops." Michael answers.

Back in the office, a terrorist comms Brianna, "We have a threat coming down the main corridor, three soldiers."

"Gun them down, no prisoners." Brianna replies.

Jaren signals his men forward and they take position behind a wall and a service desk. Jaren follows and takes cover behind the corner of an intersecting hallway.

"It's clear, sir." the soldier states, unintentionally falsely.

As he makes his move up, he missed a terrorist from behind a fountain. The terrorists shot is true and finds its mark. The other soldier regroups with Jaren. The two battle their way through a side hallway where they are met with quite a bit of enemy gunfire. Chinks of tile from the bullet-riddled walls cover the glossy floor.

The two terrorists are no match for the Ranlian Reaper, Jaren's weapon of choice. He quickly unloads a couple of grenade shots that incapacitate the villains leaving nothing but a smoke trail. Jaren and his remaining ally use the smoke cover to make their way down the hall while unloading a hail of photon bursts from their guns.

A terrorist jumps from a balcony and armed with only a knife takes down Jaren's soldier. He is wounded and down but the cut isn't fatal. Jaren takes vengeance on the terrorist with the Reaper's sickle-shaped blade and melee's him in the back.

A door in the hallway opens. It's the same door Jaren dropped off Janah. Jaren raises his gun fearing the worst. Janah pops her head out to see Jaren and rushes to hug him.

"Janah, get back in there, it isn't safe out here." Jaren demands.

"I'm coming with you. It's safer with you than in here

with a door locked. Don't bother arguing, I'm not staying behind." Janah replies.

The wounded ally guard states, "You guys make your way to the office, I'll cover your backside. I can't move right now anyway. That bastard cut me good."

"Stay alive, we'll be back for ya. We've lost too many men already." says Jaren.

Jaren and Janah have just one short hallway left before arriving. Jaren hands Janah a battle knife and a grenade.

"Just in case." Jaren says.

Janah is somewhat intimidated and fearful of just holding the weapons and gasps.

"You know what, give me that one back." Jaren says as he takes back the grenade.

"Yeah, that's probably a good idea." answers Janah.

The two take one last hug and make their way to save the senator, if he's still alive.

CHAPTER 11:

NO WATER

Danjerr has trekked his way to the rooftop of the Akyrian embassy. His Cloak of Shadows ensures his moves will go unnoticed and he easily breaches an external entrance. The remaining terrorists outside have no idea anyone has just infiltrated their guard.

Luckily for Danjerr, this vent is much cleaner and less rusty than the one he visited in The Celestial nightclub. It's even a little roomier and mush easier to maneuver. Hiding in the vents allows Danjerr to deactivate his cloaking and conserve the ionic battery. While off, the battery can recharge itself and be ready in time for the main battle, at least that is Danjerr's game plan for now.

Voices are now coming below Danjerr, it's coming from some of the black-cloaked terrorists. Danjerr can only hear two voices, but that doesn't necessarily mean only two henchman. He leans his ear to the opening. Still just two voices, followed by footsteps. Danjerr tries to peer through the vent, but it is dark as space with only a flickering light.

The battery on the Cloak of Shadows is still low. Two smoke-screen bombs remain in Danjerr's arsenal along with one concussive grenade. Danjerr must remain silent though, so the smoke screen is the only option.

Danjerr carefully places the grenade through the vent and it drops down making a clang sound loud enough to draw the attention of the nearby terrorist who turns around immediately into the smoke jetting from the grenade. Another terrorist comes up with him and they pass through the smoke screen to expect the culprit to be on the other side. However, Danjerr has out-maneuvered the ill-trained fools. Danjerr has not exited through same vent as the grenade. Rather he progressed fifteen feet down to another one. Danjerr's bet that the terrorists would enter the smoke screen paid off as he now is still separated by the screen.

Danjerr can make out the shadows cast when the light flickers and reaches for his daggers. Almost a blind shot with the darkness and smoke, but not for someone of Danjerr's experience. His attention to the shadows cast from the strobing light is all he needs. He makes his final aim and hurls the daggers at his victims. The shot is pure and final.

Danjerr notices a couple more terrorists, three more who have come around a corner about forty yards down. The terrorists reach for their Roulettes, but Danjerr's concussive grenade is already in flight and finds its mark. The concussive grenade sends out a pulse and tremor knocking out the terrorists in an instant.

Danjerr gives a half laugh and smirks while saying to himself, "Damn, I miss football. That throw would've made Favre and Namath proud."

Danjerr immediately regains focus and makes a run back for his daggers and releases them from the bodies. One from a spine, the other from the back which punctured a lung. Danjerr closes his eyes and releases a frustrated grunt. His first casualties, all due to his blades being unclean. Something Danjerr isn't used to, and doesn't want to get used to.

The good news is that no more terrorists have made their way down the hall. Their numbers are thinning in a hurry due to their under-estimation of Gellar's preparations. Danjerr knows the schematics of the embassy better than anyone other than Gellar himself. There's a shortcut to his office. Sadly, it's another vent.

"Thank God this is the last one." Danjerr says as he makes his way down to the office.

Danjerr, however, will meet more resistance than he

thought, as his concussive grenade was heard all over the embassy and caught the attention of the Pariah, Brianna Wynn.

Brianna looks over to Gellar, "That must be your friend making one of his famous grand entrances. Well, maybe I don't have time to negotiate. Looks like we'll have to take plan B and just kill you."

As Brianna raises her gun, Jaren jumps in and blasts her in the back, "Not today, you terrorist bitch!"

The remaining terrorists start a gunfight with Jaren who tries to hold them off himself. Gellar is unarmed and Janah has nothing but a battle knife. Gellar has taken cover under his marble desk.

Jaren, finds his mark on the first terrorist but must quickly take cover behind one of many pillars in Gellar's office. The remaining terrorists in the embassy filter in through the doorway that connects to the back. Easy pickings for the well-trained Captain Jaren Lee. The enemies are mowed down with only one making it through alive when Jaren had to once again take cover from fire from Brianna's bodyguards.

Janah yells from behind one of the pillar's, "Quit playing around. Blow them up!"

Jaren agrees and activates the grenade launcher of the Ranlian Reaper. He comes out from one of the pillars and blasts the door, causing it and some surrounding pillars to crack and crumble.

CLANG!

Danjerr kicks open the ceiling vent above the turmoil and drops down, but his presence is a mystery to everyone as they believe the vent came open upon the blast. Danjerr, standing at a different angle than Jaren notices one last terrorist, the traitorous Debo, still alive and whips the dagger at his chest. The dagger seems to come out of nowhere as it loses its cloaking when Danjerr releases it. The shot drives in and punctures his lungs and the traitor dies a slow death gasping for air. His body slowly falls to the floor next to where fellow betrayer Brianna Wynn lies.

"What the hell?!" shouts Jaren.

Janah rushes out inspecting the scene from afar and says, "That's one of Danjerr's daggers. How on earth did someone else get their hands on it?"

"They didn't. He's here, but for some reason he hasn't decided to reveal himself yet." Jaren replies.

Janah asks, "Reveal himself? What do you mean?"

Jaren walks over to Janah and leans in for an embrace while saying, "I'm not sure. I just know it's him. It must have been how he boarded the Avalon undetected."

"Well, whatever, let's just be glad this terrorist threat is quashed." states Janah.

There's a movement over by where Debo fell to the floor. Brianna has managed to gather enough strength from the wound that Jaren delivered earlier. Brianna lunges over and pulls the Akyrian dagger from Debo's chest. In one last shot at revenge she hurls the dagger at the couple of Jaren and Janah in embrace. The dagger makes its flight towards Janah's back as Brianna lets out one last threat, "This movement will never die!"

The threat catches their attention, but Jaren and Janah have no time to react. Both of their eyes widen fully and they clutch each other tightly gasping. As the blade reaches one foot before its destination, it has miraculously stopped. Jaren and Janah now split from each other both facing the traitor. Confusion hits the face of everyone in the room, except Gellar.

Gellar knows what has happened and furiously rushes to Brianna and clobbers her with a Stiletto he has picked up off a dead terrorist. Brianna falls hard to the ground face up. Gellar has now stepped on her throat and issues his own threat, "Your reign of terror dies here. Your radical movement dies here. And you die here."

Brianna tries to mutter a comeback, but Gellar never let's her and pulls the trigger.

BLAST!

The mystery of the stopping dagger is starting to reveal itself as it starts to tremble in the air and blood now runs down the blade and down to the floor in the form of a human body. The cloak slowly starts to deactivate itself revealing the hero. Danjerr falls to his knees and looks up at Jaren.

"Maybe now you'll believe me when I tell you I know what sacrifice is." Danjerr says while coughing blood.

"Sacrifice. Your daggers, according to you, don't kill." answers Jaren.

"They haven't been cleansed, have they Danjerr?" asks Senator Gellar.

Danjerr looks down and shakes his head sideways. Then looking back up at Jaren says, "Get Nikailyn. Get her safe. Her and other prisoners are on their stolen Dreadnought."

Jaren pauses and looks at Gellar as Danjerr now falls to the floor. Jaren says, "We'll try, but we have to secure the Citadel and clear out any remaining terrorist threat."

Danjerr responds with his last words, "Get her now. Sacrifice for me what I have sacrificed for you."

Jaren reaches for his comm, "Michael, Michael?"

Michael responds, "We've wiped out about a dozen terrorists in the rear but we couldn't get through the security door codes. However, we've spotted a Dreadnaught not far from here that we suspect could be the stolen ship."

"Good. Unfortunately, Lieutenant Debo was a double agent. The bastard stabbed us in the back, but Danjerr returned the favor." answers Jaren

"So what do you need then?" asks Michael.

"Get what's rest of the crew and make your way to the terrorist's Dreadnought if you can. There are prisoners aboard, some still alive from the fall of Minsteria, Bremmen, and Laurynie."

"Still alive?" Michael responds.

"Get there fast!" Jaren closes the conversation and puts his comm back on his belt.

Gellar looks at Jaren, "You're not going yourself?"

"We've got to secure your safety. We don't know how many terrorists are remaining." answers Jaren.

"I know Danjerr, I doubt he left any terrorist threat. I'll be alright." Gellar states as he grabs a Roulette from the floor. He looks down the barrel of both guns and then looks back over in Janah and Jaren's direction. "I'll look after Janah. You owe it to Danjerr to make sure his loved ones are safe. We'll clean up here. Then meet us at the town court."

Jaren gives Janah one last hug, "I'll be as quick as possible."

Janah responds, "Be as safe as possible."

"I will." Jaren replies.

Jaren looks at Gellar and then looks back at Janah. His legs slowly pick up speed before making his way towards the rear exit of the embassy.

CHAPTER 12:

MENDING WOUNDS

The time has passed and life is slowly returning to normal. However, today serves as a reminder for a couple parties involved in the terrorist attack. The silver lining in this dark moment in time on Metal Earth is the stronger unity now shared between the Akyrian and Oyiohan governments.

The two democracies have agreed to return to tho old political systems from before in order to avoid disgruntled extremists from going over the edge. The American Alliance will no longer alternate presidents from the two space stations, rather they will elect the new president in a popular election. Although this new philosophy isn't foolproof, there will always be a threat from evil and terrorism.

Back on Oyioh at the Citadel, President Gellar made the point clear, "Today, we start anew. I will act as a temporary president and then step down when the new president is elected. It is our hope, that the new presidential election process, like the one used by our ancestors, will bring about a stronger unity between the Akyrians and the Oyiohans instead of the rivalry that was created with the format used since the creation of Metal Earth. Let us remember this event and those who helped stop the terrorist threat and helped us unite as a people. Ladies and gentlemen, let us come together, strengthen our bonds and begin our growth as a new republic."

The large audience in the courtyard roar in approval as Gellar walks away from the podium. The improved alliance between the once bitter stations is an important asset the stations will need to move on to the new possible threat, a hostile

Ikossian government and an aggressive growing fleet of warships

and military. The missing element will become a big factor in

stopping that threat.

The mood is much different on Akyria. The Akyrians

love the new unity, but a somber setting lies at small cemetery.

Nikailyn stands beside Aren at the newest stone. The ground

freshly dug and new grass sewn. Few people are accepted into

the cemetery due to lack of space on the stations.

Nikailyn leans her head against Aren's shoulder as tears

begin to find their way out of her glossy eyes. "He'll get to find

his friend, Kellen. I guess, I guess, he , he went as he wanted,

protecting his country." says the sobbing Nikailyn.

"We'll have two very good people to look after us here. I

know we're going to miss him, but it's somewhat comforting

knowing those guys will guide us." Aren says to try and ease the

pain.

The somber pair walk up to the stone and drop some

flowers in front of it. They pause and slowly find the strength to stand up and walk away. Nikailyn again leans against Aren for strength. The two turn around and begin to proceed back to their path when they are stopped by another arrival. Jaren and Janah have made their way to pay their respects.

Nikailyn still somewhat torn at the sight of seeing them knowing Danjerr gave himself for the mission. Her last conversation with Danjerr has been longer than three years ago.

"I know you may not believe me due to our differences, but I am really sorry. Danjerr was the best type of soldier." Jaren says to Nikailyn.

"He was the best kind of brother. I just wanted to see him one more time. Promise me you won't let his death go in vain and forget everything he's done for you guys." Nikailyn replies.

"We won't. His legacy won't be forgotten." Janah answers as she puts her hand on Nikailyn's shoulder.

Nikailyn turns away and departs with Aren's arm around her. There hasn't been enough time for her to forgive the captain for forcing Danjerr to be arrested when she needed him most. She still has the bruises from her torture that reminds her of the pain from being separated from her family. It will take some time to heal those physical wounds, and perhaps longer to heal the wounds between the Ohm and Lee families.

Hopefully the families can mend like their space station counterparts of Oyioh and Akyria. All families must now unite and strengthen their alliances to defend their own loved ones against a common enemy, the impending war with the Ikossians.

CODEX:

LOCATIONS:

(alphabetical order)

Akyria: Space Station KR-7 established by the American government originally as a space
fortress but was converted to accommodate civilian life after a meteor barrage that
occurred in 2056 AD. Akyria is governed by Senator Gellar who is about to
relinquish his temporary American Alliance President status over to Senator Jopalmin
of Oyioh. Akyria is the economic power of the two stations and also boasts a much
closer resemblance of what life used to be like on earth.

Bremmen: Neighboring sector of Minsteria that was sacked by the 'Progs' shortly after Laurynie.

Celestial, The: A popular night club on Akyria where Danjerr meets many of his contacts.

Citadel, The: The military training academy on Oyioh where Jaren and Danjerr, among others,
were trained.

Faseelle: The largest sector on Akyria that serves as its capital. The nightlife is quite exotic and
vivid which is in stark contrast to the government district which is very futuristic in
architecture. It's the wealthiest Sector on any space station.

Ikoss: Space Station EK-X was the last station created by the US and was somewhat unfinished
before the Asian alliance of Russia and China purchased it. The UN didn't approve of
the buyout but has no authority in space where the Americans now run nearly eighty
percent of all economic and political situations. The UN only controls Veeson. The
Japanese spurned the offer to join and instead branched off into the other three
stations with no specific affiliation.

Laurynie: Sector south of Minsteria that was taken over by the 'Progress for Change' movement.

Metal Earth: The not-so affectionate term given to the group of space stations that is the new way
of life. "Metal Earth' was originally designed to be a space fortress by the US,

however, the plan was abandoned after the meteor attack and the satellites were
converted for civilian life.

Minsteria: Sector on Oyioh that was the home of Jaren Lee and Danjerr Ohm before there was a
takeover by the "Change for Progress" rebel group. Minsteria is in ruins now with the
lack of care and upkeep from its hostile takers. Minsteria fell after Bremmen and
Laurynie.

Oyioh: Space Station OI-0 is the sister station of Akyria. Unlike Akyria, Oyioh is mostly a
military installation with very little agriculture or plant life. Governed by Senator
Jopalmin, some of the other stations have become intimidated by his aggressive
tactics and diplomacy. Oyioh is only about two thirds the size of Akyria but is still
the second largest space station of the four.

Veeson: Space Station VS-1 was designed and built by the Americans but was given over to the
UN to use for European nations after the earth's incomplete destruction. The UN is
still a little bitter towards the American Alliance for only sacrificing their smallest
space station while keeping two and one being almost entirely comprised of the
military.

PEOPLE/GROUPS/ENTITIES:

(alphabetical order)

Brianna Wynn: Ambassador of Ikoss who has worked several shady dealings with the other space
stations in attempt to gain an advantage in economical power. Although most of the
time, the deals seem more personal than for the best of Ikoss.

Captain Jaren Lee: Jaren Lee commands the USS Avalon for the Oyioh military. The unit mostly
goes on mining expeditions to earth to strip it of resources and bring back for the
American Alliance. Jaren is engaged to Janah Omen of the Oyioh Cross-Station
Committee.

Danjerr Ohm: Former squad-mate of Jaren Lee when he served in the Oyioh military. However, he departed when he was accused of treason. He became a mercenary but worked mostly for Senator Gellar on Akyria, Oyioh's American rival station.

Janah Omen: Fiancé of Captain Jaren Lee. She is a member of the Oyioh Cross-Station Committee which is responsible for common law of the new world, Metal Earth. She highly disapproves of Jopalmin's leadership and doesn't like Jaren working for him.

Aren K'Napp: Former Oyiohan who allied with Danjerr Ohm after the Minsteria takeover. Aren and his family got split up in the scramble to find a new home in space. Aren was a former mercenary recruiter for Oyioh but shifted to Akyria when Senator Jopalmin denied his family visas traveling from Akyria to visit.

Lieutenant Debo: Senator Jopalmin's right hand man and one of the few members of the military who may know some of Jopalmin's behind-closed-doors policies.

Michael Stall: The pilot of the USS Avalon and the weapons specialist of the crew. Michael packs two dual photon pistols, or Stilettos, the standard weapon of the American Alliance Military.

Miles Sanvado: A crew member of the USS Avalon who is a no non-sense soldier who believes in no gray area in rule interpretation. Miles is Jaren's right-hand man and is responsible for the strategy behind Captain Jaren Lee's most famous battles.

MZX-20: A reconnaissance drone of Danjerr Ohm that he stole from a high-tech Asian firm (Cybernox Corp.) when he raided an underground munitions warehouse responsible for illegal weapon mods. MZX can hover and is armed with basic weaponry for defense because it is mainly used a s a scout.

Pariah: The mysterious leader of the 'Progress for Change' movement that has begun to take over sectors in Akyria and Oyioh. The identity of the Pariah is unknown.

Prime Minister Hinkle: Hinkle is only the second prime minister of Veeson. He inherited it from his father who promoted a more isolationist movement. However, this sentiment is starting to fade for some Veesonists who fear the growing threat of the Ikoss expansion and are reaching out for help.

Progress for Change: Movement started by anarchists who were bitter about losing the power
they had established on earth before the meteor strike. The radicals are extreme in
doing whatever it takes to regain its power. The leader of the group goes by the name
"Pariah."

Senator Gellar: The current President of the American Alliance. Although very conservative like
Jopalmin, Gellar isn't nearly as aggressive as Jopalmin. Gellar relies more on special
operation forces comprised of mercenaries to deal with situations since the majority of
the military is under control of Jopalmin and Oyioh.

Senator Jopalmin: The dominant senator about to attain the presidency of the American Alliance.
Aggressive and corrupt in his ways to grasp what extra power he can. He's not trusted
by any of the other stations' leaders and that includes Senator Gellar of Akyria.

WEAPONS/TECHNOLOGY:

(alphabetical order)

Akyrian Cruiser: A common stealth attack ship used by the Akyrians. The ship is more fortified
and aggressively designed compared to its Oyioh counterpart, the Oyiohan Stalker.

Akyrian Daggers: Intricate designed knives that were given to Danjerr Ohm from his friend, and
priest, Kellen Hopkins. Hopkins obtained the blades which are believed to be used
during the Crusades. The blades carry a myth that ever since they were blessed by
Kellen they have never killed. Danjerr cleans the blades with holy water after every
battle to try an maintain this belief.

Cloak of Shadows: A prototype technology Danjerr is trying out for Senator Gellar. It is the only
one of its kind, but has already proven its effectiveness.

Ikossian Dreadnought: The largest ship model in the Ikossian fleet. A couple older and smaller
versions have been know to be bought on the black market along with other Ikossian

weaponry like the Roulette photon pistol.

Ranlian Reaper: A combination of weapons in a medium sized weapon designed by Marvellen Lee, Jaren's father who was a weapon-smith. The weapon consists of a photon pistol, a grenade launcher, and a sickle like blade at the bottom of the handle. It can hold up to three grenades. It is the only weapon of its kind.

Stiletto: The name of the photon pistol which is the common weapon of the American Alliance. The black market offers illegal enhancements to the gun that make it more deadly. Ikoss offers a variation of the weapon called the Roulette. Veeson carries a version with a 'stun-only' setting called the Peacekeeper.

Titan Armor Mark IV: The latest technology in advanced shielding that is used by the Oyiohan military. The armor is ultra-flexible plating that is laced with nano- technology that will release appropriate pain killers into the wearer's bloodstream when it detects a serious blow.

U.S.S. Avalon: The ship commanded by Captain Jaren Lee and his crew. Although it's seen a large share of battles, it's mostly used as a vessel for fuel expeditions. A real shame for what remains the largest ship in the American Alliance fleet.

www.ingramcontent.com/pod-product-compliance
Lightning Source LLC
Chambersburg PA
CBHW031837170626
46807CB00004B/1495